Friends Are Very
Special People

FRIENDS ARE VERY SPECIAL PEOPLE

A Story by Lillian H. Tarry

Illustrated by Arlene Noel

Hallmark Children's Editions

Friends Are Very
Special People

One day I was playing in my yard. I was bouncing my red ball as high as I could make it go. But I bounced it the wrong way and it went over the fence into the yard next door. The new boy lives there. He saw the ball land and brought it back to me. He stayed and we played together for a while. His name is Joey.

I like Joey. I think he likes me.
He helped me carry my rocking horse
into the yard so I could go for a ride.

Another time, I gave him my
black crayon when he
broke his, so he could finish
drawing a picture of his house.

One day some big girls laughed
at me because I had freckles.
Joey looked angry at them
and took me to his tree house.
"I think your freckles
are nice," Joey told me.

When some boys pushed Joey off his
bike that afternoon, I washed his knee
and put a bandage on it
and told him how brave he was.

Joey likes secrets and so do I.
I showed Joey a seashell I had hidden
in a box in my closet.

My grandmother sent it to me.
Joey said he wouldn't tell anyone about
my seashell because friends keep secrets.
I showed him how to put it to his ear
so he could hear the ocean waves.

Joey doesn't like to play dolls,
and I don't like to
play cowboys and Indians!

But he doesn't mind playing house
if he can be the Daddy. I'm the Mommy
and the kittens are the children.

For our pretend dinner, Mommy
gave us some cookies. Joey and I
each wanted the last cookie.
When he grabbed it, my pretty plate
fell on the floor and broke. I cried
and said he couldn't play
at my house any more.
But Joey said he was sorry
and he didn't mean
to break the plate. It was
an accident. So I said,
"Oh, that's all right."
Then we were friends again.

When Joey and I
went for a walk in the park
we met a little girl named Kate.
Kate was crying because
she had lost her dime in the sandbox.
We helped her look for it.
I found a broken bracelet.
Joey found a sock
and a toy rubber tire.
Then Kate found the dime
in the pocket of her dress
and we all laughed.
She hadn't lost her dime at all!

We liked Kate. One day all three of us
went outside after a rainstorm.
We saw the birds shake the water off
their wings and begin to sing again.

We puckered our mouths and
tried to sing the way the birds sing.
But we couldn't do it and we
laughed at the funny sounds we made.

It was Kate who first
saw the rainbow.
"Look at the rainbow,"
she said to Joey and me.

We all stopped laughing
and looked at it
for a long, long time
without saying anything.

Oh, friends are very,
very special people—

like Kate, Joey and me.